Santa Claus is Coming to The Town

Written by: **Thomishia Booker**

For Carter
and
Truly

It is the time of the year where we spread joy and Christmas cheer!

We know Santa Claus is coming to The Town
with our favorite red nosed reindeer.

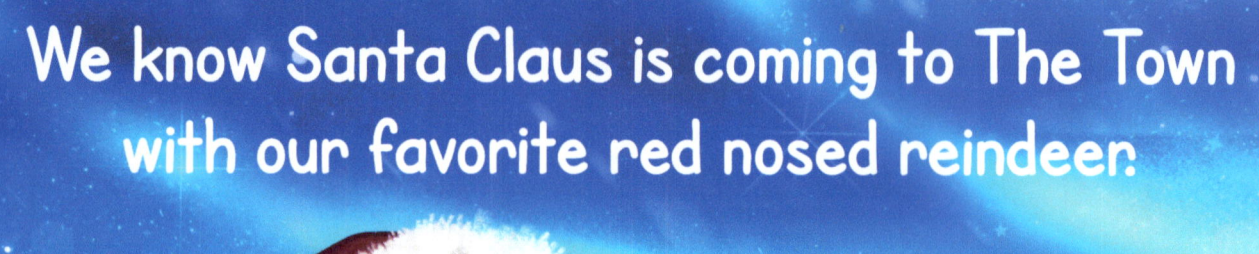

He will be dressed in all red with
a toy filled sack.
You will know it is him by his
boots that are shiny and black.

Some call him Santa and others call him Saint Nick. Flying all around the world in one night is his very best trick.

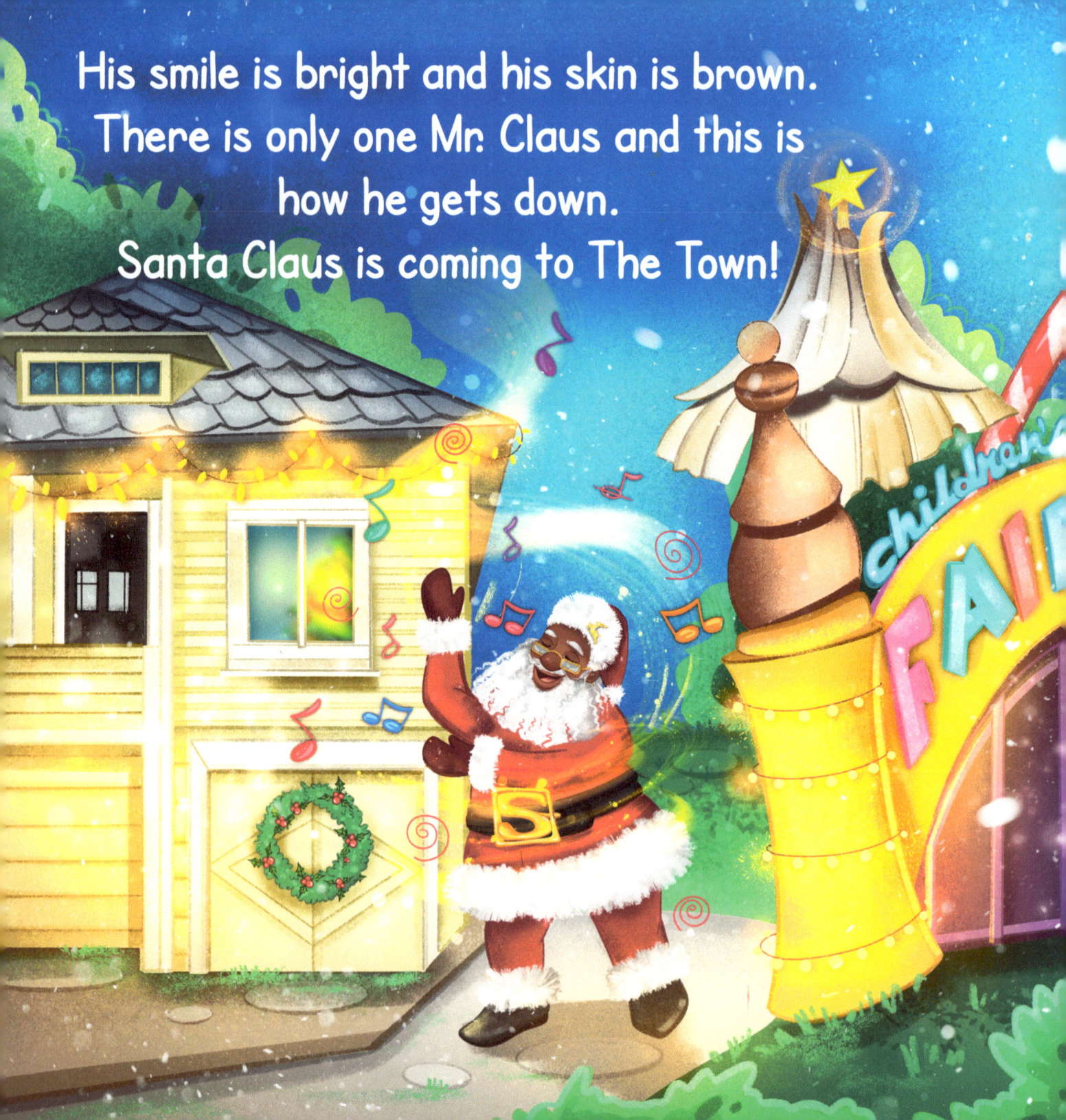

His smile is bright and his skin is brown.
There is only one Mr. Claus and this is
how he gets down.
Santa Claus is coming to The Town!

He does a little dance as he slides through the door.

He must be very careful to avoid dropping presents on the floor.

He is giving out gifts with
the flick of his wrists.
There is no need to
worry because you have
already made his list.

...Bay
...nt.
...ntion,
you might miss him... ...ght.

the
ng for.

There will be candy canes, gum drops and chocolate galore.

He will fly over Lake Merritt on the way to your house.
Everyone will be sleeping including your pet mouse.

Happy thoughts of Christmas will fill your dreams as you lay nestled in bed.

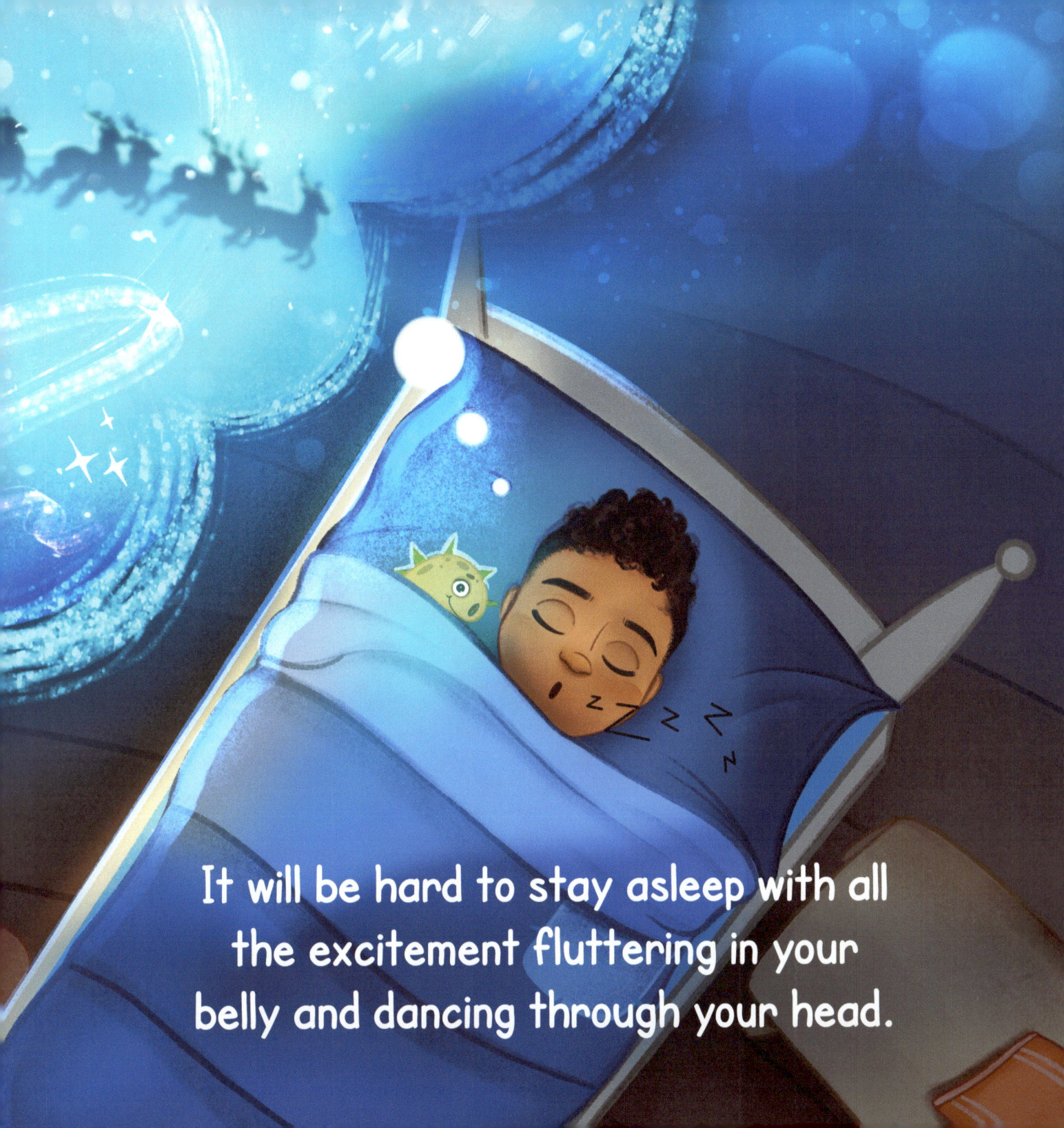

It will be hard to stay asleep with all the excitement fluttering in your belly and dancing through your head.

Santa Claus will be here soon so get in bed and sleep tight.
Merry Christmas to all and to all a good night.